# Pink Tiara Cookies for Three

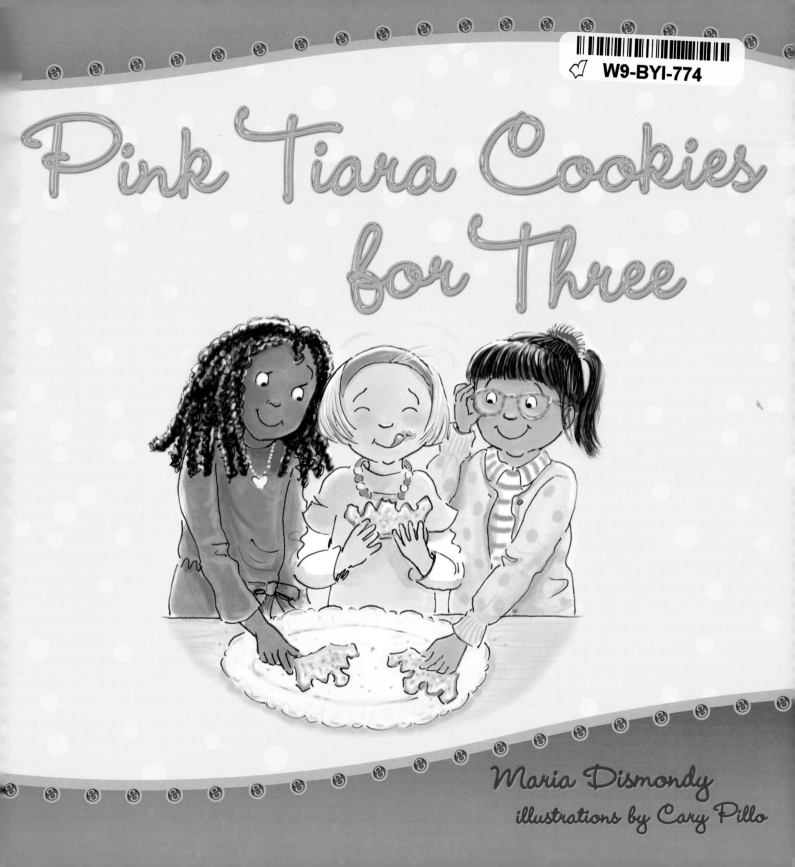

Maria Dismondy

illustrations by Cary Pillo

First Printing 2012
All rights reserved.
Printed in the United States of America

Summary: Sami and Stella are best friends and neighbors. When Jasmine moves in across the street, a friendship triangle begins. The girls learn how to adjust and make room for one more.

Dismondy, Maria Cini (1978- )
Pink Tiara Cookies for Three
1. Friendship  2. Self-Esteem  3. Individuality  4. Character Traits  5. Mental Health  6. Child Development  7. Bullying
9. Inclusion

ISBN: 978-0-615-51620-2

Library of Congress Control Number: 2011912877

Making Spirits Bright: One Book At A Time
An imprint of Maria Dismondy Inc.
5449 Sylvia
Dearborn, MI 48125
www.mariadismondy.com

With love, to my two little miracles . . .

Ruby and Leah

**Note to Families:** As an author, it has been my goal to spread the message of bullying to as many children as possible. This book brings up the concept of "Three's a Crowd." Children have the tendency to exclude others and may directly or subtly threaten their friends, which is a form of bullying. As family members, you can help your child learn what they can do in this type of a situation. Try role-playing scenarios with your children. Teach them how to appropriately be assertive. Keeping the lines of communication open in your family will allow your children to come to you when they need help. You want your children to learn to solve their own problems, but oftentimes they need coaching at home. Visit www.mariadismondy.com for more information on character development.

*I would like to give thanks to the talented and dedicated individuals who helped bring this book to life: Cary Pillo, the very talented illustrator, my editor, Kathy Hiatt, the staff at Worzalla Publishing, Steve Brennan for his creative logo design, my attorney Matthew Bower, Bernadette Szost for her connections as an illustrative agent, the staff at Red Line Editorial for their impressive design work, Sami Dynda for her personal story that led to this idea, and above all, my husband Dave and daughter Ruby for their patience and support when mama is crazy busy working on a new book!*

Everything was perfect for Sami before Jasmine moved in. Sami loved school. She had her favorite teacher and her best friend, Stella, who lived right next door. Now Jasmine lived across the street and she was ruining everything.

"Sami, remember there's always room for one more. Think about giving Jasmine a chance. I know it's always hard with three," Mama said. "We used to call it a friendship triangle because two would play and one would always be left out. You and Stella need to figure this out," Mama preached as Sami complained once again about Jasmine.

"I already have Stella to play with, Mama. Stella and I are like mittens. We're a pair. We don't need anyone else. Mittens only come in pairs. With one more, someone gets left out. Besides, we like anything pink and we share all our jewelry."

"Plus, we have our song, Mama," Sami began to sing.

*Cookies, candy, chocolate cake.*
*We're best friends for goodness sake!*
*Jump rope, swings, and hopscotch, too.*
*There's so much we love to do!*
*Stella and Sami singing by the tree,*
*Mittens come in pairs, just you and me!*

Just then, the doorbell rang. It was Stella and Jasmine.
"Hi Sami. We're playing school. Do you want to play
with us?" Stella asked.

"Well, who do I get to be?" asked Sami.

"Jasmine is going to be the teacher this time," Stella
whispered.

"But I'm always the teacher. She doesn't know how to be the teacher like I do! Stella, you can't be my best friend anymore if you keep playing with Jasmine!" Sami whined, as she turned and ran up the stairs.

The next day at recess, Sami sat down and Jasmine joined her. Jasmine leaned over and asked, "Stella invited me over to play after school today. She said we would make her mom's famous pink tiara cookies. Do you want to come?"

Sami didn't reply. She was furious. Stella was her best friend. Sami was the one who always made the famous pink tiara cookies with Stella and her mom. She didn't want to share her with Jasmine. Was this ever going to end?

Sami stood up to find Stella. She spotted her on the swings and ran as fast as she could to get to her. Before she could get to Stella, Jasmine took the only swing left.

Sami played alone that day. She always had Stella to play with and never had to worry about making new friends. Sami thought about how she and Stella had made up their own special song to sing on the swings. She decided playing alone was no fun at all.

Sami saw Stella alone, so she walked up to her and said, "Because of Jasmine, I had to play all alone today. I feel like I'm being left out," Sami pleaded.

"Well Sami, it's not fun for Jasmine to play alone either. She's new and doesn't know anyone. You could have played with us," Stella declared.

Back in the classroom, the teacher announced,
"Children, I am choosing your partners for science
today. Jasmine, you will partner up with Sami."

"Ugh!" Sami groaned.

Sami and Jasmine worked on the assignment silently. The teacher gathered the children to go over the answers to the experiment. "Sami, are mammals warm-blooded?"

"Um . . . no?" Sami answered nervously. The class laughed. *I wasn't even paying attention*, thought Sami. *I was too busy thinking about how I wanted Stella as my partner.*

Jasmine tried to help and chimed in, "What she meant to say is yes, mammals are warm-blooded." She smiled at Sami.

After class, Sami found an empty swing next to Stella.
*Finally*, she thought to herself. Jasmine walked up to them.
Sami remembered how she felt when she played alone.

"Hey, do you want to swing with us?" asked Sami.

"What should we do? There are no more swings," Stella whispered.

"There's always room for one more. Let's go over to the tire swing so we can all swing together," said Sami. Jasmine smiled. Sami smiled too.

"Hey, Stella, let's teach our song to Jasmine but change the words a little bit!" The girls walked away, holding hands as Sami sang:

*Cookies, candy, chocolate cake.*
*We're best friends for goodness sake!*
*Jump rope, swings, and hopscotch, too.*
*There's so much we love to do!*
*Stella and Sami singing by the tree,*
*Mittens come in pairs and now there are three!*

In the end, **Sami** was still **Stella's** friend and she had a new friend, too. She learned that she didn't have to lose her best friend to make room for one more.

Sami was excited to tell her Mama about how she solved the friendship triangle problem. But before she could, there was a knock at the door. Standing before her were Jasmine and Stella with a plate full of the famous pink tiara cookies.

Photo courtesy of
Christina McGuire Photography

This is the third children's book from beloved children's author Maria Dismondy.

As a teacher, author, and much sought after presenter, Maria saw a need for a children's book that dealt with the difficulty kids have when they are grouped in threes. She also wanted a book that offered dessert. With those things in mind, *Pink Tiara Cookies for Three* was born.

This award-winning author and dynamic speaker presented to more than 10,000 children at various venues in one month alone. She is driven to spread her message on bullying and empowering children to face challenges and to do the right thing. Maria holds degrees in education and child development. She makes her home in southeastern Michigan with her husband, Dave, and their daughters, Ruby and Leah.

To find out more, visit www.mariadismondy.com

Cary Pillo grew up in a small town nestled near the foot of the Cascade Mountains in Washington State. She spent her childhood riding her bicycle, drawing, and building forts in the forest. Cary attended Washington State University and majored in Fine Arts. She has illustrated numerous articles, educational materials, and books for children. She lives in Seattle with her husband and a mischievous fox terrier named Atlas. Cary still rides her bike and draws but prefers hiking in the forest instead of building forts.